WORKING WITH

TRANSPORT

Sonya Newland

KID ENGINEER

WAYLAND
www.waylandbooks.co.uk

First published in Great Britain in 2020 by Wayland

Copyright © Hodder and Stoughton, 2020

Produced for Wayland by
White-Thomson Publishing Ltd
www.wtpub.co.uk

FSC
www.fsc.org

MIX
Paper from
responsible sources
FSC® C104740

Credits
Editor: Sonya Newland
Illustrator: Diego Vaisberg
Designer: Clare Nicholas

Every attempt has been made to clear copyright. Should there be any
inadvertent omission please apply to the publisher for rectification.

Printed in China

Wayland
An imprint of
Hachette Children's Group
Part of The Watts Publishing Group
Carmelite House
50 Victoria Embankment
London EC4Y 0DZ

An Hachette UK Company
www.hachette.co.uk
www.hachettechildrens.co.uk

! All the materials required for the projects in
this book are available online or from craft or
hardware stores. Adult supervision should be
provided when working on these projects.

3 Cut two more strips of magnetic tape, the same length as the cardboard, and stick them on the outside edge of each 0.5 cm line. Leave a 1 cm gap between the strips.

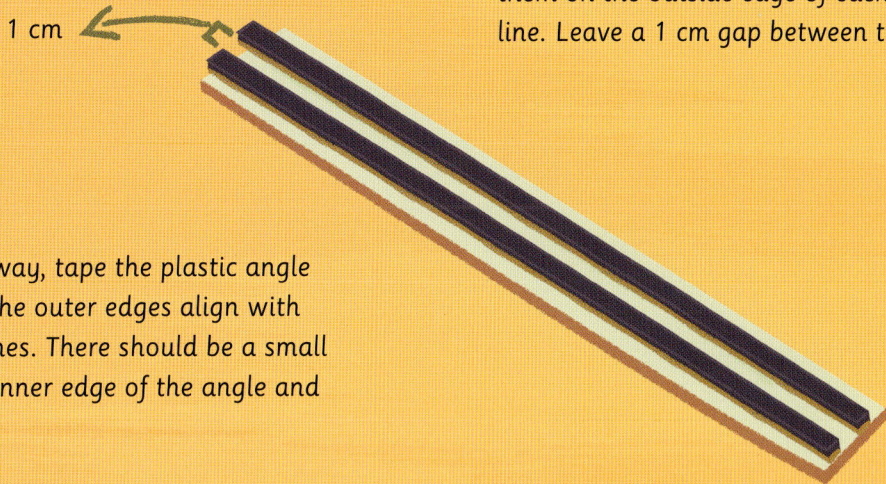

1 cm

4 To create the guideway, tape the plastic angle mouldings so that the outer edges align with each of the outer lines. There should be a small space between the inner edge of the angle and the magnetic strip.

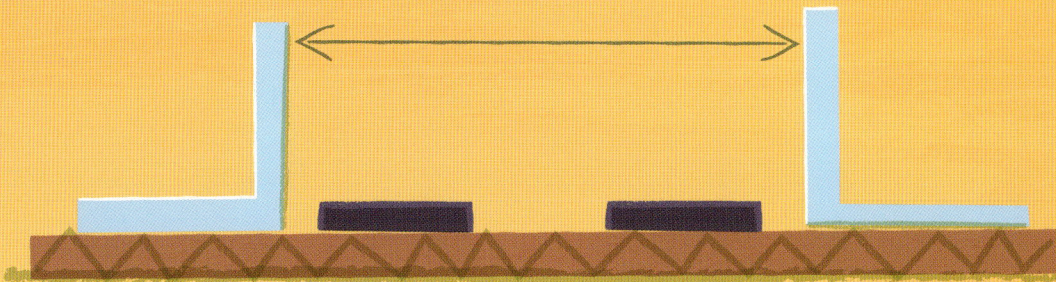

5 Put your train on the track, with the magnetic strips facing downwards. It should hover above the tracks below, with a small space on either side. You should be able to slide it along the track.

TEST IT!

Measure the distance between the train and the track, then experiment with different train weights. Put coins on the train and see what happens to the distance between the train and the track. Do the weights make it easier or harder to move? What do you think would happen if you used stronger or weaker magnets?

MARINE ENGINEERING

Boats are huge and heavy. Marine engineers have their work cut out designing vehicles that can that travel safely and swiftly across oceans and seas.

Ship shape

People who design ships are called naval architects. They have to consider many different things:
- Materials must be strong but light enough to float, as well as rust-resistant.
- The shape must be streamlined so the ship can move easily through the water.
- The design needs to cater for passengers or cargo, and weight must be carefully distributed.

SORTED!

Isambard Kingdom Brunel (1806–59) was a great British engineer who designed bridges, tunnels and ships. The SS *Great Britain* was a miracle of 19th-century engineering. In 1843, it became the first propeller-driven iron ship to carry passengers across the ocean.

The SS *Great Britain*'s screw propeller was cutting-edge ship-building engineering at the time.

The bow is shaped in a peak to slice through air and water.

The bridge offers a wide view to help sailors navigate clearly.

The funnel releases waste gases from the engine.

The anchor can be lowered to hold the ship in place.

The propeller turns to move the ship forward.

The rudder can be moved from side to side to steer the ship.

Deep down

Submarine engineers face even bigger challenges. A submarine has to be really strong to withstand the water pressure deep under the sea. It must move quickly but stealthily. Submarines stay underwater for months at a time, so engineers have to plan for fuelling and keeping submariners entertained all that time!

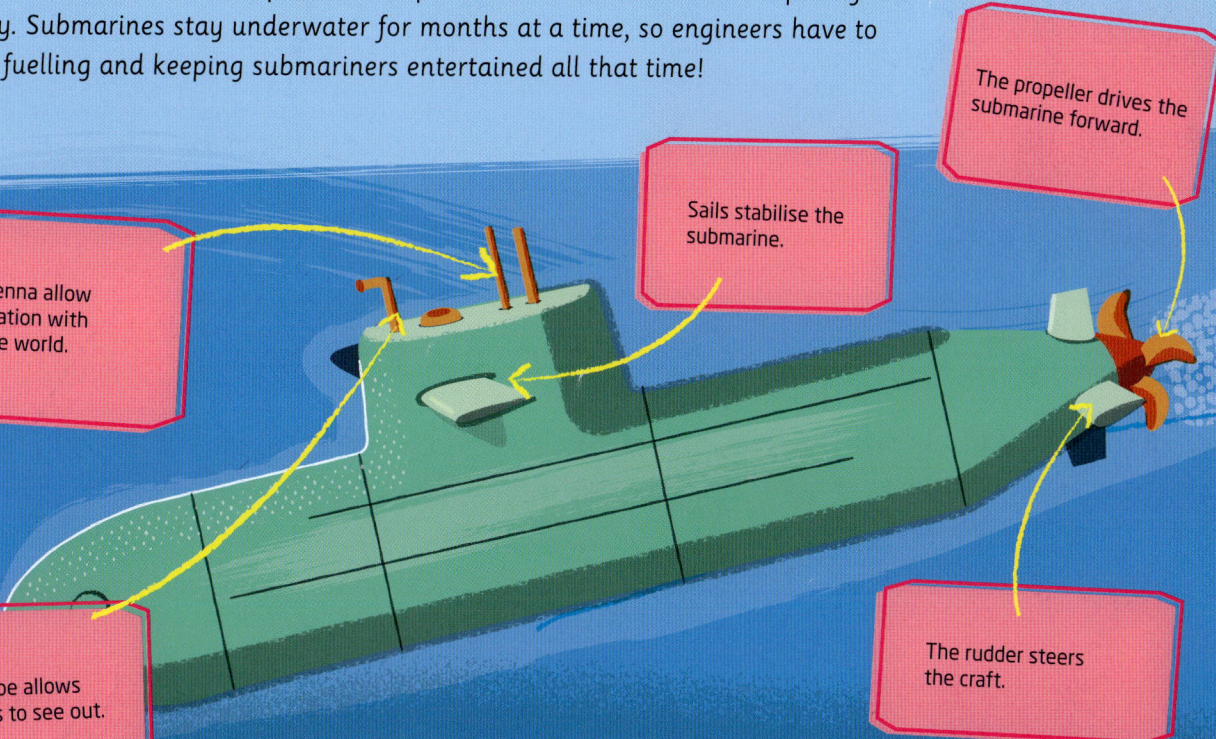

The propeller drives the submarine forward.

Sails stabilise the submarine.

Radio antenna allow communication with the outside world.

The periscope allows submariners to see out.

The rudder steers the craft.

YOU'RE THE ENGINEER: DESIGN AN UNSINKABLE SHIP

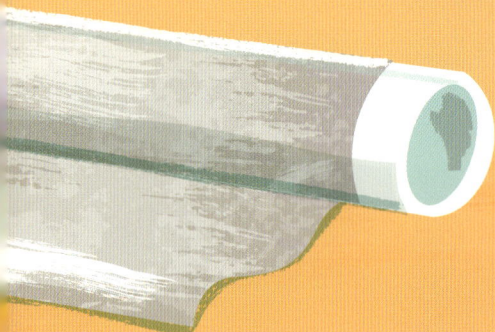

How do engineers design ships that can travel quickly while carrying heavy loads without sinking? Find out for yourself by constructing a strong, safe boat.

You will need

Tin foil
Scissors
A large tray of water
Small coins such as 1p or 5p pieces
Fan or hairdryer

1 Cut a piece of tin foil about 15 cm by 10 cm and fold up the edges to create a rectangular 'boat'. Put it in the tray of water.

2 Place the coins in the boat one at a time. How many can you place before the boat sinks?

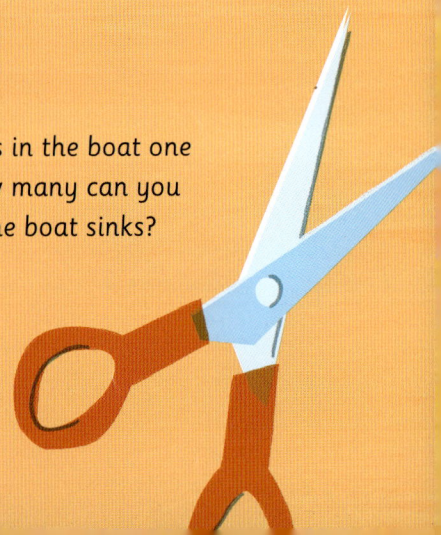

3 Remove the coins and dry them. Repeat the experiment, but this time think carefully about where you can place each coin. Does placing them differently affect the strength and stability of your boat?

4 When you have created and tested your first boat, create two more boats – one larger and one smaller. Experiment with different weights and distributions.

5 Finally, try changing the amount of water in the tray. Try deep, shallow and medium amounts. Which is the best combination of water depth, size and distribution to keep your boat afloat?

TEST IT!

When you have finished working with weights, try thinking about the *shape* of your boat. Fold the foil into different shapes and see which one is the strongest and most stable. Blow it across the water using a fan or hairdryer!

AERONAUTICAL ENGINEERING

Look up at the sky – what can you see? A passenger plane? A police helicopter? A drone? All these machines that fly within Earth's atmosphere are designed by aeronautical engineers.

How air moves

All aeronautical engineers have to understand aerodynamics. This is the science of how air moves things around … and moves around things! Forces have to work in particular ways for an aircraft to move.

Streamlining

The shape of an aircraft is very important. Engineers design planes with streamlined shapes. Long bodies and pointed noses create less air resistance, so the plane can fly faster.

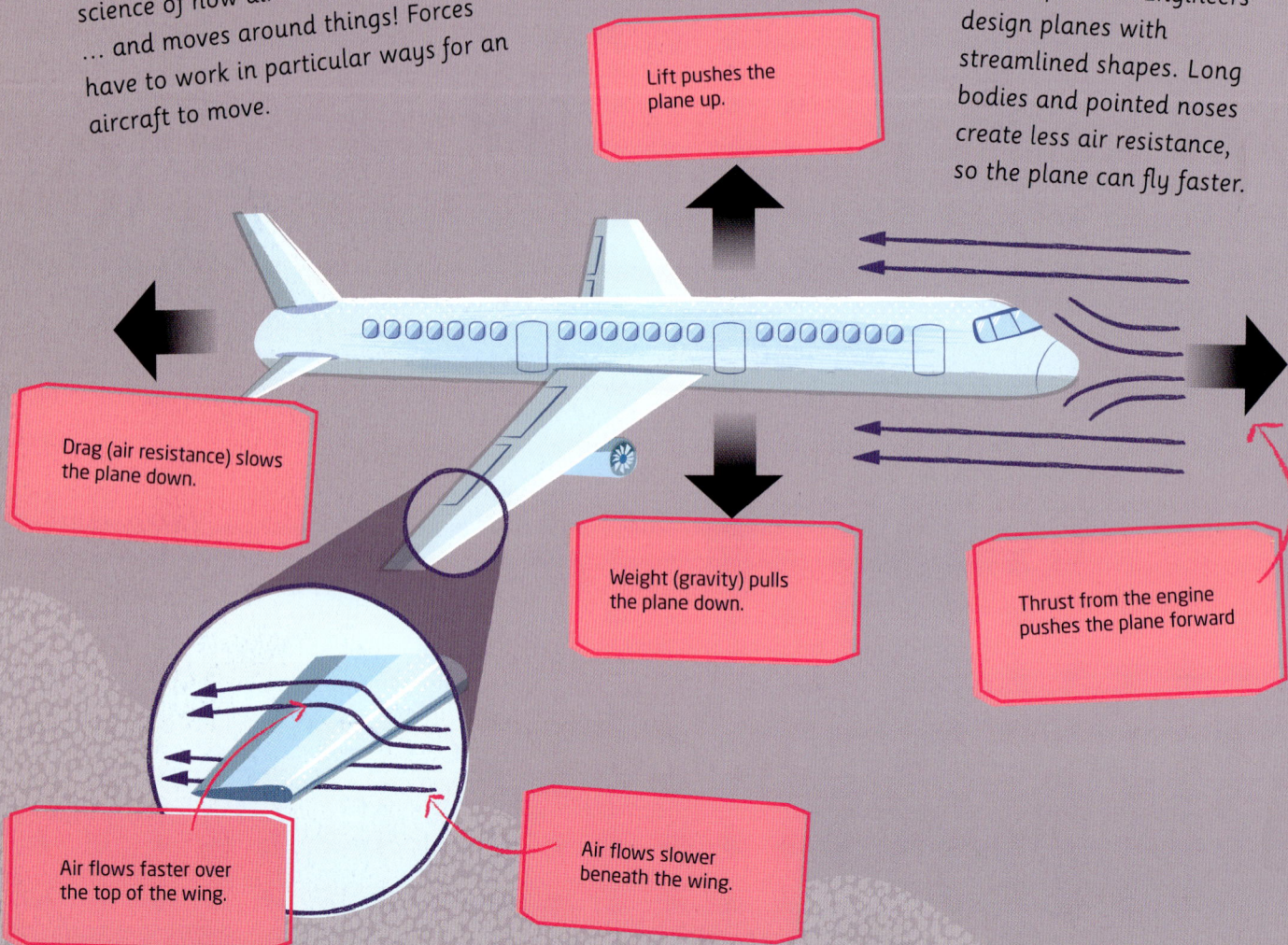

Lift pushes the plane up.

Drag (air resistance) slows the plane down.

Weight (gravity) pulls the plane down.

Thrust from the engine pushes the plane forward

Air flows faster over the top of the wing.

Air flows slower beneath the wing.

Swift and stealthy

Military aircraft are engineered to have special capabilities. They might have to fly *really* fast or be able to duck and dive nimbly. They are equipped with stealth technology, which allows them to fly undetected.

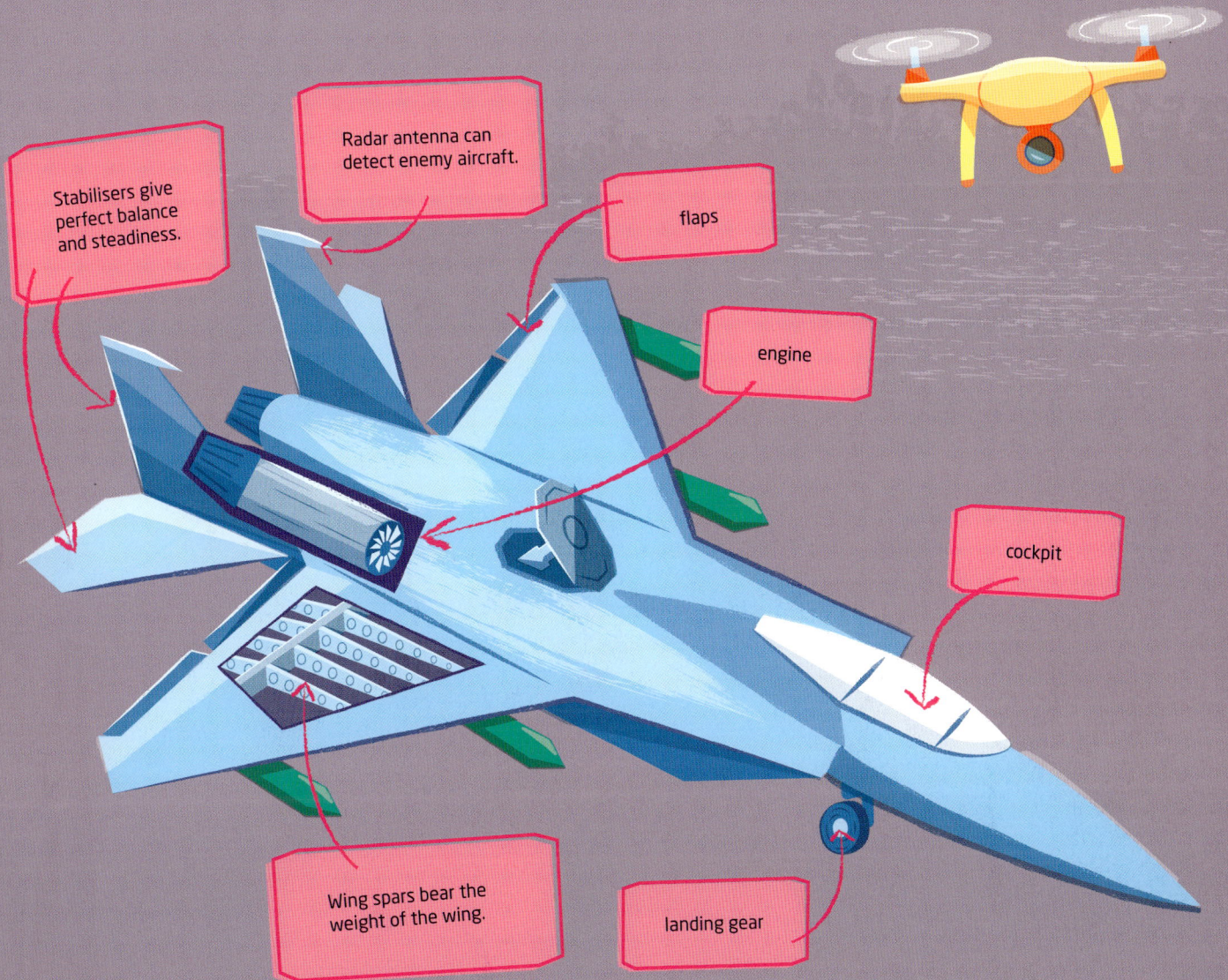

Stabilisers give perfect balance and steadiness.

Radar antenna can detect enemy aircraft.

flaps

engine

cockpit

Wing spars bear the weight of the wing.

landing gear

Engineers are also responsible for **planning** all the **incredible infrastructure** that aircraft rely on, such as **airports** and systems of **runways.**

SORTED!

The first supersonic plane was the Bell X-1, engineered by Bell Aircraft, which made its first flight in 1946. It was described as 'a bullet with wings'! Its special 'all-flying' tail, which could move in different directions to help stabilise the plane, was powered by a rocket engine.

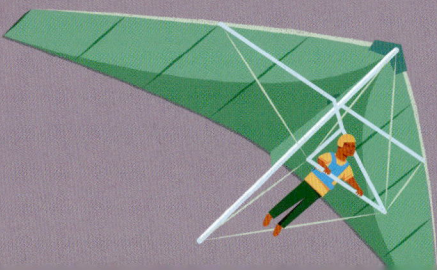

BLADES, NOT WINGS

Helicopters are odd-looking aircraft. Their shape doesn't seem very aerodynamic! That's because they are engineered differently from planes.

How does a helicopter work?

A plane gets its lift (see page 18) from air rushing across the surface of its curved wings. A helicopter generates lift through its spinning rotor blades.

When hovering, the combined forces of lift and thrust have to equal the combined weight and drag so the helicopter stays still.

When moving, the forces of lift, drag, weight and thrust operate the same as on a plane.

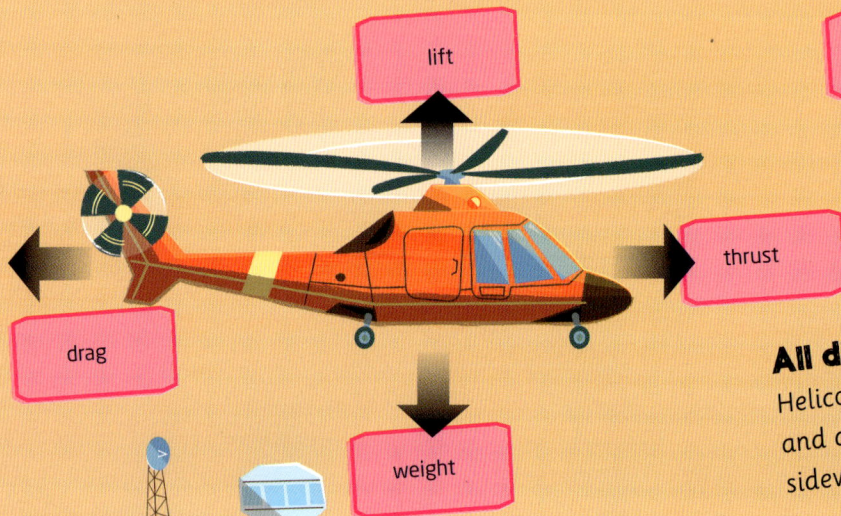

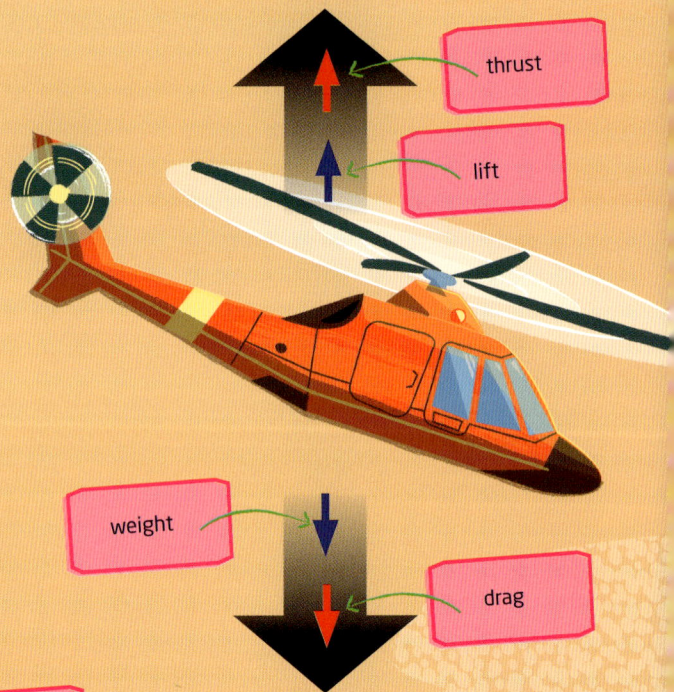

thrust

lift

weight

drag

lift

thrust

drag

weight

All directions

Helicopters can move straight up and down. They can fly backwards, sideways, or hover in one spot.

Special-purpose aircraft

Helicopters can land just about anywhere so they are often used by the military and for rescue missions in tough environments. Engineers are constantly finding ways to improve helicopters for their particular purposes, by making them lighter or more manoeuvrable, for example.

The helicopter can hover and steer thanks to short rods attached to each blade.

The rods connect to a swash plate that can tilt and move.

The rotor blades are attached to a rotating mast.

'Nautical' refers to boats, so aeronautical and astronautical engineers design and build 'flying boats'!

21

YOU'RE THE ENGINEER: SET A HELICOPTER SPINNING

Get to grips with how helicopters work by engineering your own rubber-band helicopter!

You will need

A plastic propeller
Sticky tape
A craft stick
A paperclip
Thin coloured card
Scissors
Two rubber bands

1 Tape the propeller to one end of the craft stick.

2 Bend the paper clip so the smaller (inner) curve is at a right angle to the larger, outer section.

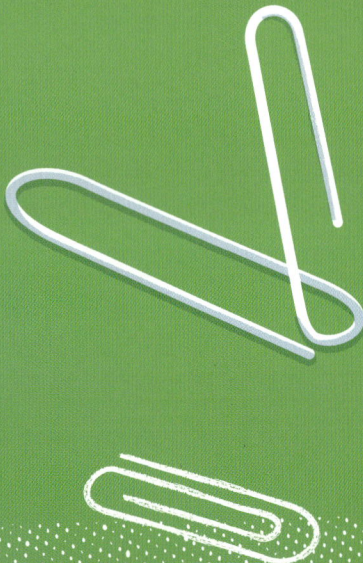

3 Attach the paperclip to the bottom of the craft stick. Tape the larger section to one side. Shape the smaller section so it makes a hook on the other side.

4 On the coloured card, draw the shape of a helicopter body (the cabin and tail) about 12 cm long. Cut this out carefully and stick it to the craft stick, just below the propeller.

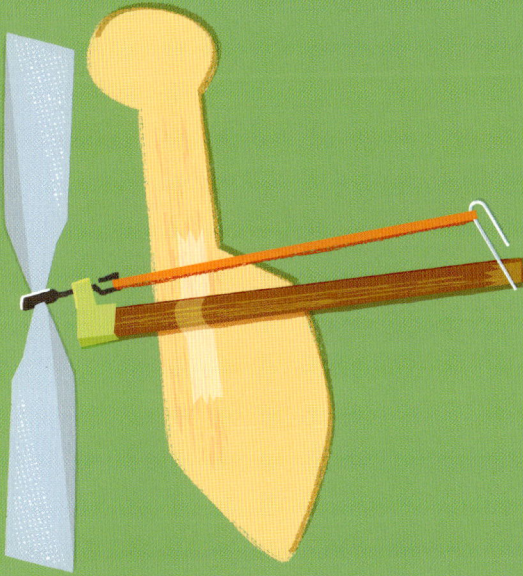

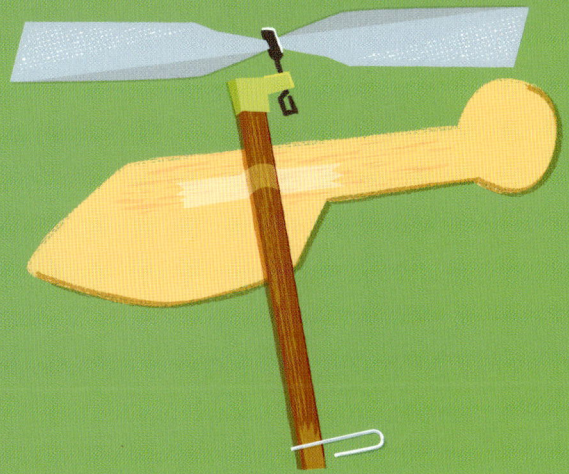

5 Take one rubber band and loop it around the hook on the propeller at one end and the sticking-out bit of the paperclip at the other. Do the same with the second rubber band.

6 Turn the propeller blades until the rubber bands are quite tightly twisted. To fly your helicopter, hold the top of the propeller and the bottom of the craft stick, then let go of the top first and the bottom straight after. Watch it fly!

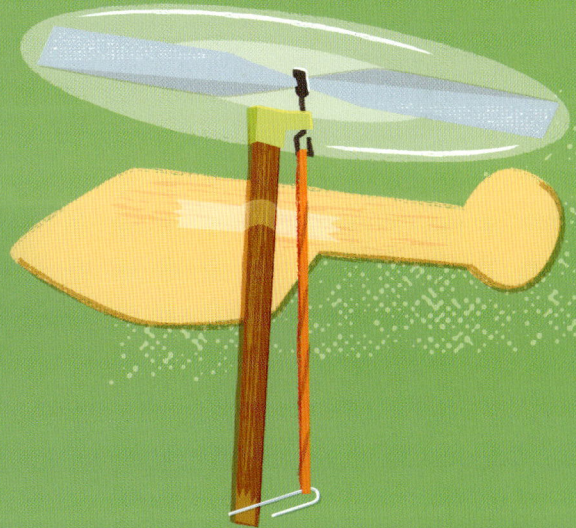

TEST IT!

When you have practised releasing your helicopter a few times, try 'throwing' it slightly as you let go. What effect does this have? Now try adapting the design of your helicopter. What features could you add to give it greater stability?

ROCKET SCIENCE

Astronautical engineers are a type of aerospace engineer. But rather than designing aircraft that fly close to Earth, they create incredible machines that travel in space.

Satellites orbit in Earth's atmosphere. They are used for communication and global positioning systems (GPS). The batteries, computers and thrusters are built into a platform called a bus. Satellites are powered by solar panels.

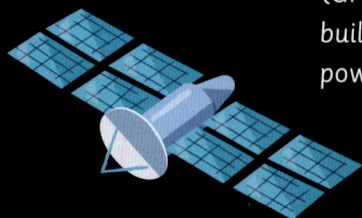

Rockets are designed to launch other vehicles such as satellites or manned spacecraft into space. Rockets are powered by jet engines. They are engineered to blast off with enough energy and speed to escape the pull of Earth's gravity.

Probes are unmanned spacecraft that travel deep into space. They investigate other planets in the solar system, using the very latest engineering techniques and technology. Engineers design them to survive the most extreme conditions.

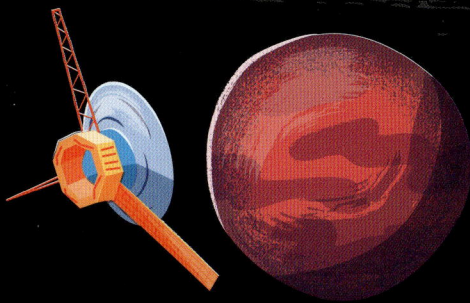

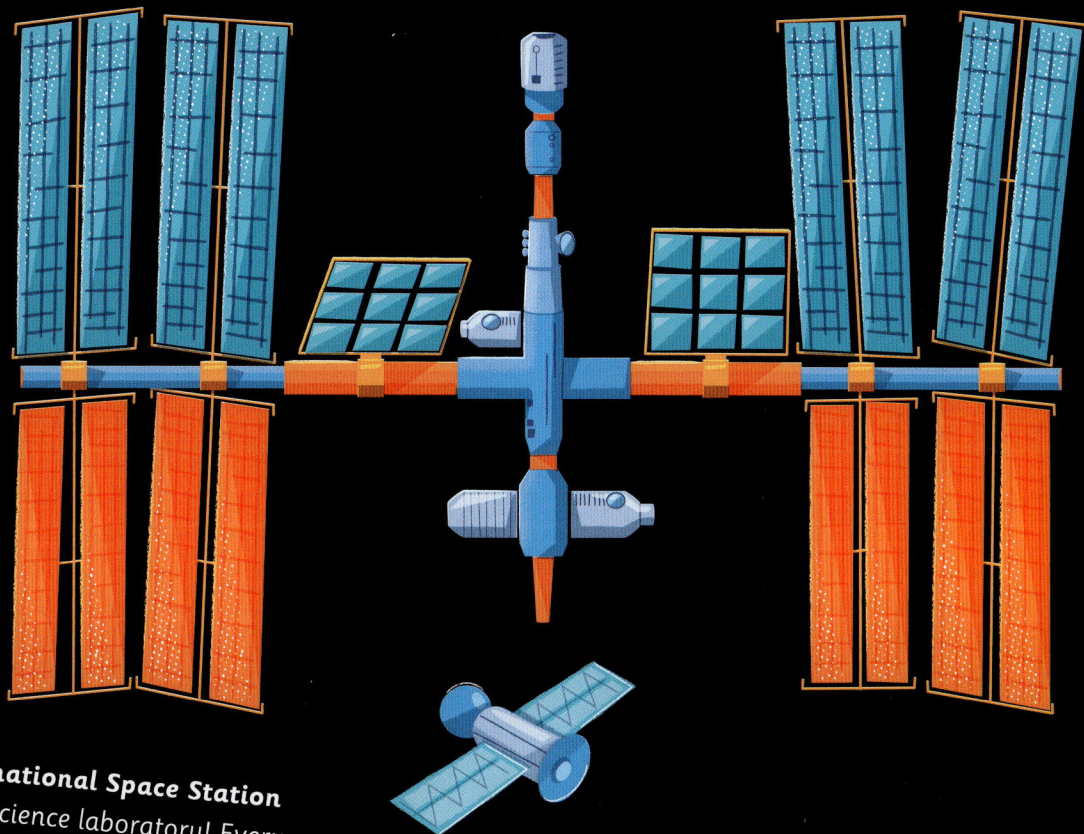

The International Space Station is a huge science laboratory! Every part was designed so that it could be constructed out in space. More than 50 computers control the systems on the station. It is home to between three and six astronauts at a time, who carry out experiments on living in space.

YOU'RE THE ENGINEER: LAUNCH A ROCKET

Find out what forces astronautical engineers have to consider by building and blasting off your own rocket.

You will need

An empty 2-litre plastic bottle
A piece of thin card
Sticky tape
Some cardboard
Scissors
A cork that fits the bottle
A pump with a needle connector

1 Make the nose of the rocket by rolling the piece of card into a cone and sealing it with sticky tape. Attach it to the bottom of the bottle.

2 Cut the cardboard into three right-angled triangles and stick them at equal distance around the top of the bottle. These are your rocket's fins.

3 Fill the bottle about one-quarter full of water and put the cork in the neck of the bottle. Make sure it's tightly sealed!

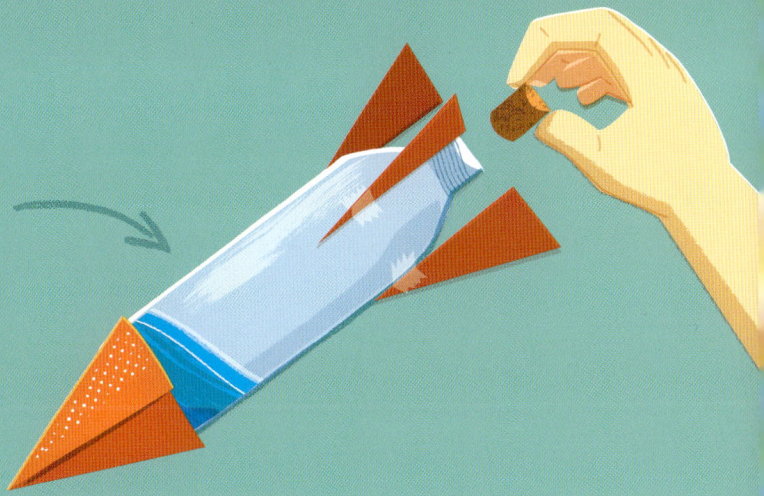

4 Ask an adult to help you push the needle of the pump through the cork so that it goes all the way through to the inside of the bottle. Then put your rocket on the ground outside, ready for launch. Make sure it is pointing away from people!

5 Slowly pump air into the bottle. Notice how the water starts filling with air bubbles. Keep pumping until the rocket takes off!

TEST IT!

Time how long it takes from when you start pumping to when the rocket blasts off. Make a note of how high and how far your rocket travels. Then repeat the rocket launch using different amounts of water. Try filling the bottle one-third and then half-full of water. What difference does it make to your measurements in terms of time, height and distance?

THE FUTURE OF TRANSPORT

Humans will always want to travel farther and faster. So, transport, aerospace and infrastructure engineering are likely to evolve and improve.

Smart roads

Clever cars need clever roads – and 'smart roads' are already being built in many countries. These intelligent transportation systems use the latest technology, such as sensors and solar panels, to make driving safer and easier.

traffic-light timings decided by how much traffic there is

street lighting powered by solar panels

Space tourism

Going to space for a holiday isn't the stuff of science-fiction any more – it is now a main focus for aerospace engineers. One day, perhaps you'll holiday on the Moon!

Environmental issues

Finding ways to make vehicles more energy-efficient is a top priority for transport engineers. Will hybrid or electric cars (see page 7) be the most environmentally friendly cars of the future? Or will engineers discover new, even cleaner ways of powering vehicles?

What will they think of next?

Engineers are also working to improve car design. They are developing vehicles that can cross the most challenging terrains. They have even created 'autonomous vehicles' – cars that can drive themselves!

charging points for electric cars widely available

apps show when the next bus will arrive

GLOSSARY

aeronautical describing things related to travel in the sky within Earth's atmosphere

alloy a mixture of two or more metals

architect someone who designs buildings or other structures

astronautical describing things related to space travel

automotive describing things related to motor vehicles

axle a rod that goes through the middle of a wheel, which spins around

bodywork the metal outer shell of a car

chassis the base frame of a vehicle

combustion engine an engine that converts heat energy into mechanical energy to power a vehicle

diesel an engine that burns a special type of heavy oil

fossil fuel a fuel such as coal, oil and natural gas, which is formed from the remains of plants and animals

global positioning system (GPS) a system that uses signals from satellites to pinpoint where a user is

gravity a force that pulls two objects towards each other

infrastructure the basic structures and facilities that a society needs to function, such as roads and power supplies

levitation when something rises up and hovers in the air

locomotive the part of a train that contains the engine

magnetism a force caused by moving electrical charges

manoeuvrable able to be moved around easily in different directions

periscope a device made of tubes and mirrors that allows you to see over the top of obstacles

streamlined describing something that is shaped to move easily through air or water

supersonic describing something that can travel faster than the speed of sound

FURTHER INFORMATION

Books

Transport (Building the World) by Paul Mason (Franklin Watts, 2019)
Vehicles (Adventures in STEAM) by Georgia Amson-Bradshaw (Wayland, 2019)
Space (Adventures in STEAM) by Richard Spilsbury (Wayland, 2019)
Trains, Planes and Ships (Awesome Engineering) by Sally Spray
(Franklin Watts, 2019)
Spacecraft (Awesome Engineering) by Sally Spray (Franklin Watts, 2019)

Websites

https://www.youtube.com/watch?v=erYf6NNw8Ec
Watch this ten-minute video all about transportation engineering.

https://www.esa.int/kids/en/news
Visit the European Space Agency's website and find out all the latest on space
travel and transport.

http://www.da-vinci-inventions.com/davinci-inventions.aspx
Find out more about the machines designed by Leonardo da Vinci – one of the
greatest engineers who ever lived.

INDEX

SERIES CONTENTS LIST

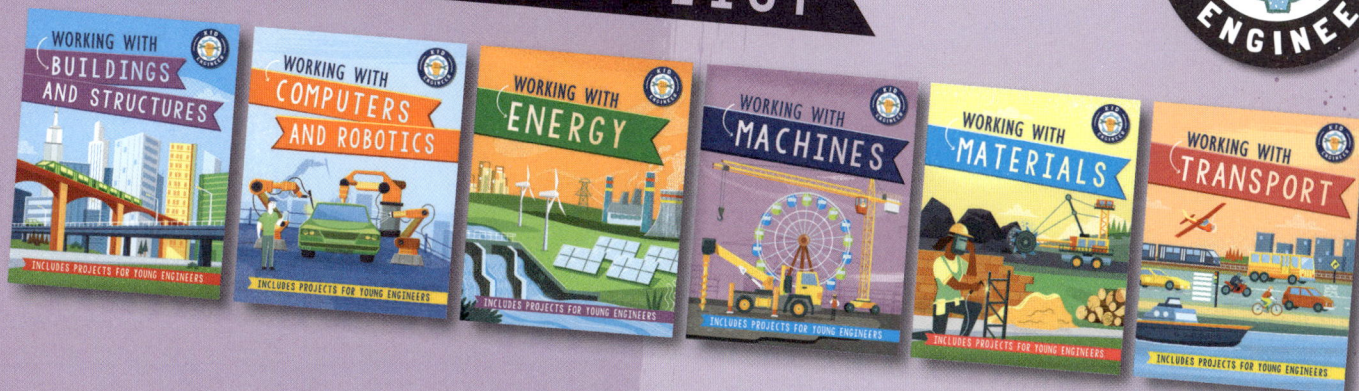

Working with Buildings and Structures

Engineering buildings and structures
Forces at play
You're the engineer: Take the paper
    building challenge
Building materials
Arches and domes
You're the engineer: Make a geodesic dome
Skyscrapers
Bridges
You're the engineer: Build bridge models
Tunnels
Moving and shaking
You're the engineer: Test buildings in jelly
Amazing buildings and structures

Working with Computers and Robotics

Rise of the machines
Hardware and software
You're the engineer: Binary beads
Printed circuit boards
Big data
Amazing algorithms
You're the engineer: Understanding
    algorithms
Helpful robots
You're the engineer: Build a brushbot
Where humans can't go
You're the engineer: Robotic arm
Artificial intelligence
What does the future hold?

Working with Energy

Energy engineering
Electricity
You're the engineer: Test electrical circuits
Fossil fuels
Hydropower
You're the engineer: Build a water wheel
Geothermal energy
Wind power
Solar power
You're the engineer: Make a solar oven
Biomass
Saving energy
You're the engineer: Test insulating
    materials

Working with Machines

Mechanical engineering
Work, force and movement
Levers
You're the engineer: Lever experiments
Pulleys
You're the engineer: Build a pulley system
Wheels and axles
You're the engineer: Working with wheels
Inclined planes and wedges
Screws
You're the engineer: Archimedes' screw
Complex machines
Powerful machines

Working with Materials

What are materials?
Properties of materials
You're the engineer: Testing properties
Friction
You're the engineer: Racetrack friction
Metal
Plastic
You're the engineer: Create a new plastic
Glass and ceramics
You're the engineer: Changing clay
Wood and textiles
Materials of the future
You're the engineer: Engineering structures

Working with Transport

Get a move on!
Automotive engineering
You're the engineer: Build a balloon car
Railway engineering
You're the engineer: Make your own Maglev
Marine engineering
You're the engineer: Design an unsinkable
    ship
Aeronautical engineering
Blades, not wings
You're the engineer: Set a helicopter
    spinning
Rocket science
You're the engineer: Launch a rocket
The future of transport

WAYLAND
www.waylandbooks.co.uk

CONTENTS

GET A MOVE ON!

Think of all the different ways we get around – by car, bus, train, plane ... and more! Transport and aerospace engineers are the people who design and build the vehicles and infrastructure that keep us on the move.

On the road

From transit vans to supercars, automotive engineers consider lots of things when designing a vehicle. How and where will it be used? What should it be made of? How will it be powered?

RAILWAY ENGINEERING

Railway engineers design and build engines and carriages. They also plan and run whole rail networks, from the tracks and signals to the mechanical and electrical systems.

Old and new

The first trains were steam locomotives. Engineers designed them with coal-powered boilers. Today, most trains are either diesel or electric.

Many passenger trains are driven by electricity.

The electric current may come from overhead cables or from a special 'third rail' on the track.

Passenger trains are often long and very fast.

Diesel locomotives are driven by a diesel engine.

The engine moves the wheels by turning gears.

Many diesel trains are freight trains, carrying goods or cargo. They need more powerful engines to pull the heavy weights they carry.

3 Tape the straws widthways to one side of the card, about a quarter of the way in from each end. Attach the wheels to the axles by pushing the lids securely onto the ends of the ink cartridges that are sticking out of the straws.

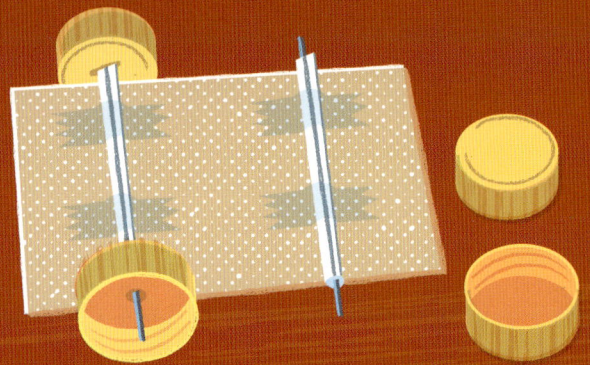

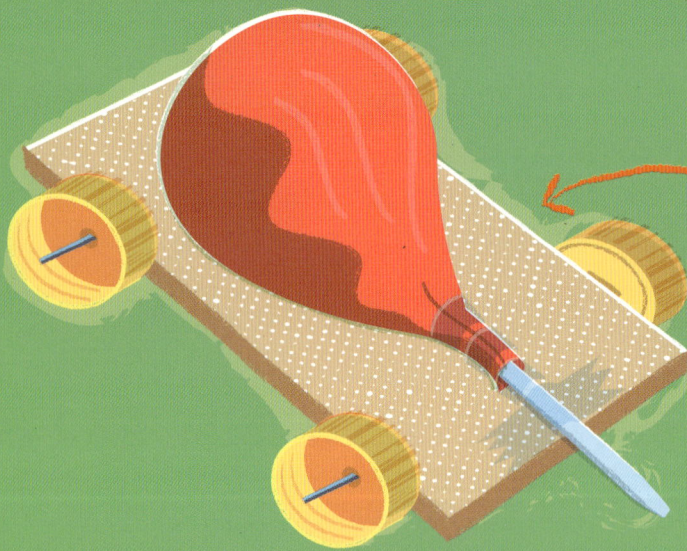

4 Put the neck of the balloon over the end of one of the plastic pen cases. Secure it with tape. Then tape your balloon 'engine' to one end of the cardboard.

5 Blow up the balloon through the pen case. Keep your finger over the end until you're ready to let the car roll!

TEST IT!

Try adapting the design of your car to make it go faster or travel over different surfaces. Use buttons or bottle tops of different sizes and styles for the wheels. Make the body out of different materials to experiment with different weights. Try different body shapes, too.

YOU'RE THE ENGINEER: BUILD A BALLOON CAR

Tackle the challenges of automotive engineering by assembling the components to build a balloon car.

You will need

Four plastic bottle lids
A hammer
A nail
Two biros
Two straws
A piece of card (about the size of a playing card)
Sticky tape
A balloon

1 Get an adult to help you make a small hole in the middle of each bottle lid using a hammer and nail. These will be your wheels.

2 Take the plastic ink cartridges out of the biros. Cut the straws so they're slightly shorter than the ink cartridges, then slide the cartridges inside the straws to make your axles.

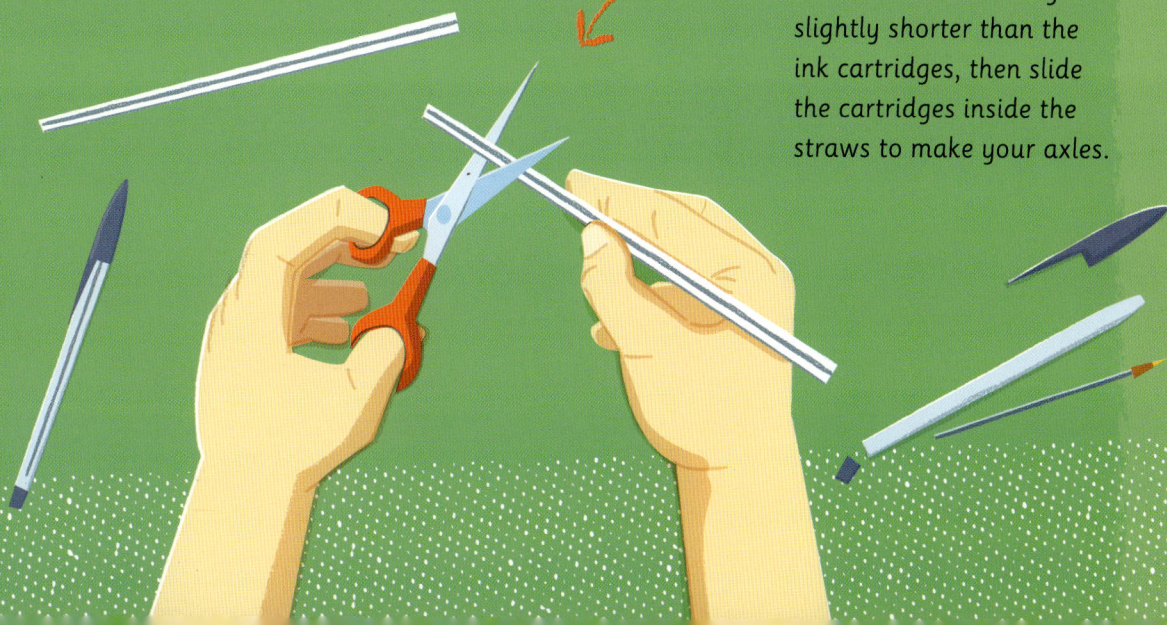

1980s

2000s

Traffic engineers design and build systems such as coordinated **traffic lights** that help traffic move **safely and efficiently.**

Green cars

Vehicle exhaust fumes pollute the air and contribute to global warming. Today's engineers are designing more environmentally friendly cars. Hybrid cars have two power sources – an internal combustion engine and an electric motor. Electric cars are powered by batteries.

Inside and out

Automotive designers have to think about how both internal and external features work.

The battery powers the electrical systems such as lights and starter motor.

The steering column allows the driver to change direction.

The exhaust system removes gases from the car.

chassis (the base frame)

The suspension is a system of springs and shock absorbers joined to the tyres.

brakes

AUTOMOTIVE ENGINEERING

Automotive engineers design, test and build all the different components that make up road vehicles. They consider everything from the tyres, to the engine, to the bodywork.

1960s

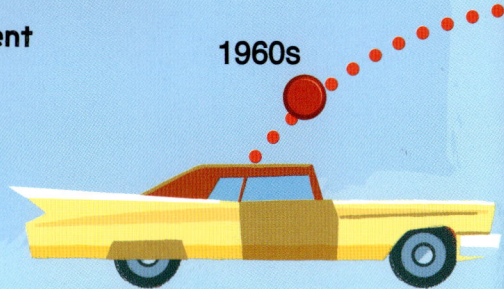

Cars through time

Car design and engineering has come a long way since German engineer Karl Benz invented the Benz Patent Motorwagen in 1886 ...

1940s

1886

1920s

The engine powers the vehicle.

lights

Safety first

Roads are busy and dangerous places, so safety is a key concern for auto engineers. They design systems to make vehicles safer. These might be improved safety belts or bumpers. Or they could be super-strong frames that can protect passengers in a crash.

tyres

Off road ...

Transport and aerospace engineers don't just design everyday vehicles. What do you think engineers might have to think about when designing ...

a quad bike?

an airship?

a tank?

Reach for the stars

Have you ever dreamed of going to space? Astronautical engineers make that dream a reality. They create manned and unmanned spacecraft that put humans in space and explore other worlds.

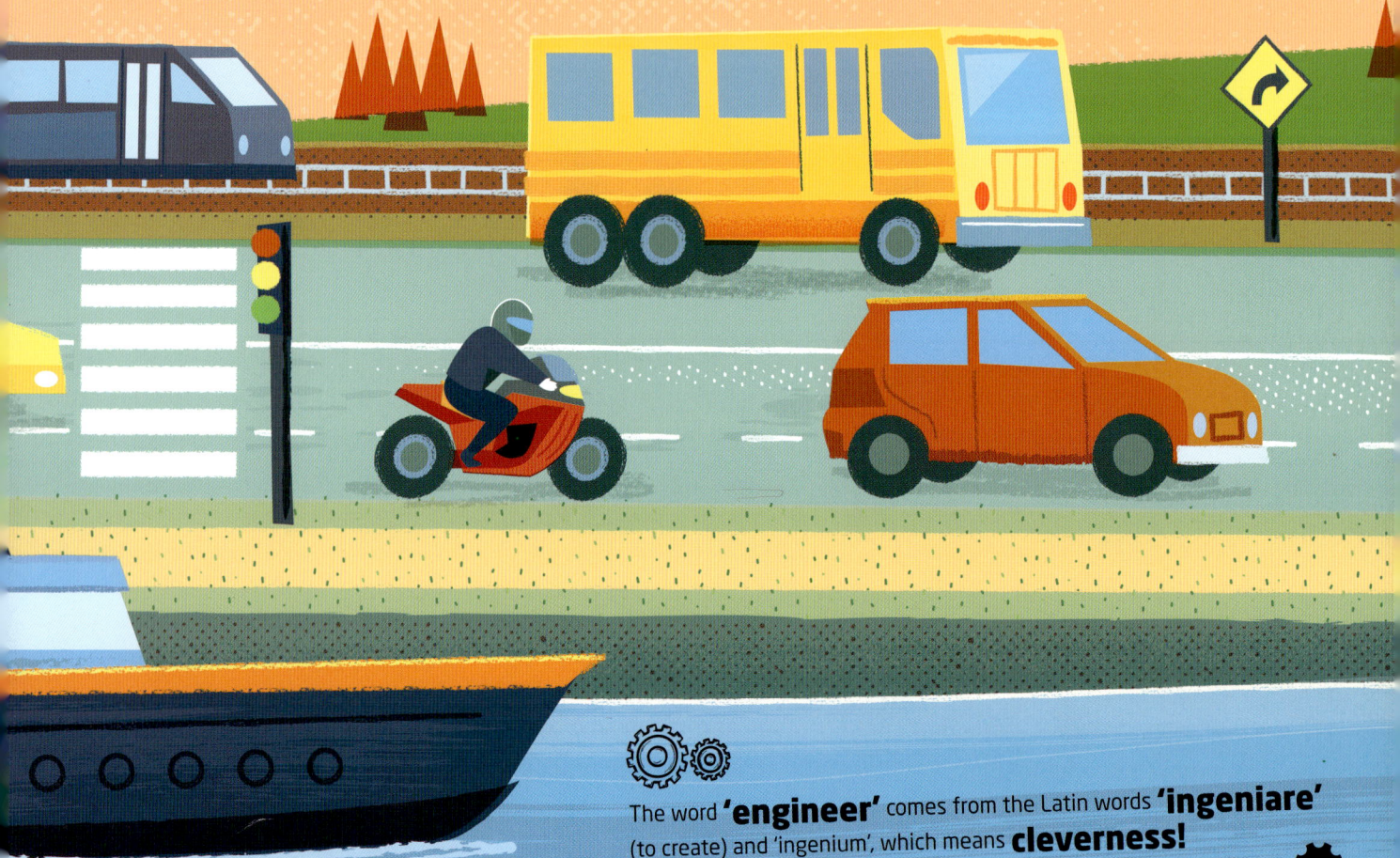

The word **'engineer'** comes from the Latin words **'ingeniare'** (to create) and 'ingenium', which means **cleverness!**

YOU'RE THE ENGINEER: MAKE YOUR OWN MAGLEV

See how engineers harness the power of magnets to design a train that moves on air!

You will need

Magnetic tape
A rectangular block of wood
    (approx. 10 cm x 3.5 cm)
A piece of thick cardboard
    (approx. 25 cm x 8 cm)
A pencil
A ruler
Two pieces of angle moulding
    (approx. 25 cm long)
Sticky tape

1 Cut two pieces of magnetic tape of 10 cm each. Stick them to the wooden block (your train) so they run along each long side of it.

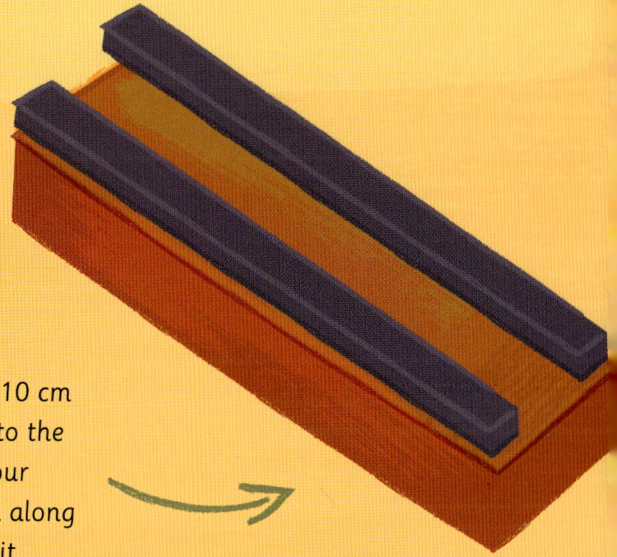

2 On the piece of cardboard (your track base), draw a line lengthwise right down the middle. Draw two more lines 0.5 cm out from either side of the centre line. Then draw two further lines 2 cm out from the centre line.

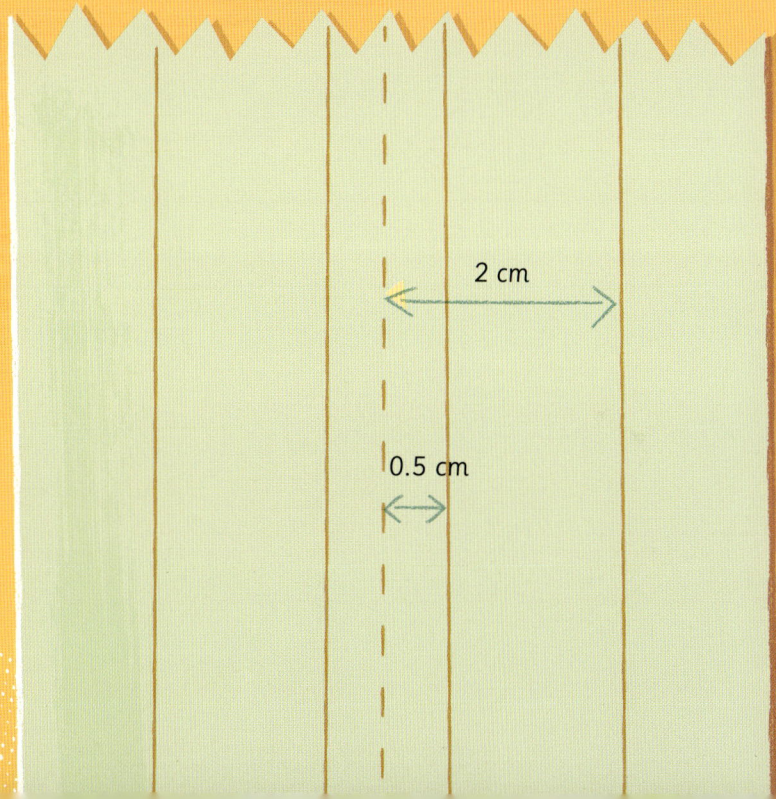

2 cm

0.5 cm

Off the rails

The Maglev ('magnetic levitation') train is a special, super-fast train. It has no engine. It works thanks to amazing electrical engineering and magnetism. The Maglev is better for the environment than electric or diesel trains because it doesn't rely on fossil fuels for power.

SORTED!

British engineer George Stephenson (1781–1848) is known as the 'father of railways'. He came up with the idea of a rail gauge – a fixed distance between rails on the track. This meant that all trains could be designed to run on the same tracks. Stephenson's gauge is still the standard all over the world.

The **Shanghai Maglev** is the **fastest** train in the world. It can travel at up to **430 km/h.**

Maglev carriages are made of a special aluminium alloy, which makes them lighter than normal train carriages.

Large magnets are fixed under the train.

The track is called a 'guideway'.

Magnetised electric coils on the guideway repel the magnets under the train.

The train is lifted ('levitated') a little way above the beams.